MW01174244

Earth's Amazing Animals

CORE CONTENT LIBRARY

ANIMAL
TOP
10

Animal Athletes

Joanne Mattern

RED CHAIR
·PRESS·

Earth's Amazing Animals is produced and published by Red Chair Press:

Red Chair Press LLC   PO Box 333   South Egremont, MA 01258-0333

www.redchairpress.com

Publisher's Cataloging-in-Publication Data
Names: Mattern, Joanne, 1963–
Title: Animal top 10. Animal athletes / Joanne Mattern.
Other Titles: Animal top ten. Animal athletes | Animal athletes | Core
content library.

Description: South Egremont, MA : Red Chair Press, [2019] | Series:
    Earth's amazing animals | Includes glossary, Power Word science term
    etymology, fact and trivia sidebars. | Interest age level: 007-010. |
    Includes bibliographical references and index. | Summary: "If there
    were Animal Olympics, some animals would be gold medal winners! Which
    animal could compete in synchronized swimming? Which animal would win
    gold in the marathon?"--Provided by publisher.

Identifiers: LCCN 2018955617 | ISBN 9781634406932 (library hardcover) |
    ISBN 9781634407892 (paperback) | ISBN 9781634406994 (ebook)

Subjects: LCSH: Animal locomotion--Juvenile literature. | Animals--
    Juvenile literature. | CYAC: Animal locomotion. | Animals.

Classification: LCC QP301 .M38 2019 (print) | LCC QP301 (ebook) | DDC
    591.47/9--dc23

Illustrations by Tim Haggerty.

Photo credits: cover, pp. 1, 5 (top, bottom), 6–9, 13, 15, 19, 21–24, 28, 31–39
iStock; pp. 3, 5 (center), 12, 14, 29–30 Shutterstock; p. 10 © Peter Harry Lee/
Alamy; p. 11 © Stephen Dalton/Minden Pictures; p. 16 © Markus Varesvuo/
Minden Pictures; p. 17 © SCOTLAND: The Big Picture/Minden Pictures; p. 18
© Guy Edwardes/Minden Pictures; p. 20 © Michel & Gabrielle Therin-Weise/
Alamy; pp. 25, 27 © blickwinkel/Alamy.

Printed in United States of America

0519 1P CGF19

Table of Contents

Introduction. 4

And the Winners Are... 5

#10: The Chameleon 6

#9: The Spinner Dolphin 8

#8: The Desert Locust. 10

#7: The Pronghorn Antelope 13

#6: The Gannet 16

#5: The Jaguar 19

#4: The Kangaroo 22

#3: The Horned Dung Beetle 25

#2: The Froghopper 28

#1: The Cheetah. 32

Animal Athlete Runners-Up 38

Glossary. 39

Learn More in the Library 39

Index 40

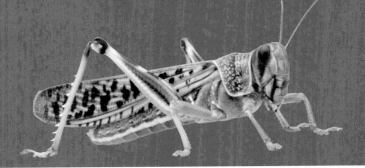

Introduction

Athletes **compete** in many different ways. Some are strong. Others are super-fast. Still more are great at jumping, swimming, or boxing. Others are great at hitting a target.

Just like people, many animals are athletes too. But while people usually compete to win a game or just have fun, animal athletes have a different goal. Many animals use their athletic skills to survive. An animal that is a fast runner or a strong fighter has a better chance of staying alive. Strong, fast animals can catch **prey**. Other animals use their speed or skill to stay away from **predators** and escape death.

We've put together a list of the Top Ten Animal Athletes. Take a look and see why these animals are the fastest, strongest, and most athletic creatures on Planet Earth!

And the Winners Are...

Here are our choices for the Top 10 Animal Athletes. Turn the pages to find out more about each of these Olympic-worthy creatures.

10. The Chameleon

9. The Spinner Dolphin

8. The Desert Locust

7. The Pronghorn Antelope

6. The Gannet

5. The Jaguar

4. The Kangaroo

3. The Horned Dung Beetle

2. The Froghopper

1. The Cheetah

#9

#8

#2

10 The Chameleon

Some people are sharpshooters. They try to hit a target with an arrow or a gun. The chameleon may be the best sharpshooter of the animal world. And this creature's weapon is its tongue!

Chameleons are lizards with some very interesting body parts. One of the most interesting is the animal's tongue. A chameleon is one to two feet (30–60 cm) long, but its tongue is about twice that long. The chameleon keeps its tongue curled up in the back of its mouth. But when an insect flies past—zap! The chameleon uncurls its tongue and shoots it out of its mouth at lightning speed.

The chameleon's sticky tongue grabs an insect and yanks it back for a tasty snack!

Power Word: Chameleon is a word with Greek and Latin roots meaning ground lion. (Some thought the lizard's neck flap looked like a lion's mane.)

9 The Spinner Dolphin

Have you ever watched synchronized swimming? That's when a group of swimmers spin and move through the water doing exactly the same moves at the same time. Spinner dolphins could definitely get an Olympic medal for that sport. These animals like to swim in groups. They often jump out of the water and spin around.

It's a Fact

Spinner dolphins live in water, but they are mammals, not fish.

Maybe spinner dolphins are just having fun when they leap and spin.

A spinner dolphin starts its spin under the water. Then it bursts out of the water and leaps into the air. A dolphin can spin five or more times before it falls back to hit the water with a loud slap. A dolphin can even flip itself head-over-tail in the air!

Scientists aren't sure why spinner dolphins like to spin. They may be communicating with each other. They may be trying to remove **parasites.**

8 The Desert Locust

Long jumpers run and jump as far as they can. Many animals are great at the long jump. One of the best is the desert locust.

Locusts are a type of grasshopper. They usually live in the deserts of Africa and Asia. However, sometimes these insects **swarm** over large areas of land. They are big eaters. A swarm of millions of locusts can eat all the crops in an area in just a few minutes.

Swarms of desert locusts have been written about for thousands of years.

Desert locusts are great jumpers because they have long, strong back legs. The locust uses those legs to push off the ground with tremendous force. A desert locust can jump more than three feet (1 m). That distance is more than 20 times its body length. If a person did that, he or she would be able to jump about 120 feet (36.5 m). And the locust doesn't even have to run up to the starting line to begin its jump.

It's a Fact

Desert locusts are also good at flying long distances. Swarms have flown from Africa to England and even to the Caribbean Sea. That's thousands of miles!

7 The Pronghorn Antelope

The pronghorn antelope is the second-fastest animal on land. This animal can run up to 60 miles (96 km) an hour. It can also run at a steady speed of about 30 miles (48 km) an hour over a long distance, which makes it a top animal athlete. A pronghorn could run a **marathon** in just 45 minutes. It would take even the fastest human more than two hours to complete the race.

Pronghorn antelope live in North America. They are much faster than any predators in their **habitat**. Scientists think the antelope developed its super speed to outrun predators that are now **extinct**.

The pronghorn antelope has several special body parts that help it run so fast. Its heart is larger than normal, which allows extra blood to flow to the antelope's body. Its lungs are also larger to allow the animal to get more oxygen into its body. The antelope also has padded toes to take in the shock of hitting the ground. And its hair is hollow, which makes its body lighter.

Even baby pronghorns can run super-fast. Females give birth to one or two fawns in the spring. The fawns hide in the long grass until they are fast enough to run away from predators like bobcats, coyotes, and golden eagles. By the time the fawns are a week old, they can run faster than most people.

Pronghorn fawns

6 The Gannet

How do you get your
dinner when it is
far below you? You
dive! A sea bird called
the gannet is a champion
diver. These birds fly in huge
flocks high over the oceans,
looking for schools of fish to
eat. When their super-sharp
eyes spot the fish, the gannets
go into action. The birds tuck
in their wings, point their
heads down, and dive.
By the time they hit
the water, the birds'
wings are flat against
their bodies. The
school of fish doesn't
know what hit it.

It's a Fact

A gannet usually swallows its prey underwater to avoid another bird grabbing the fish out of its mouth.

A gannet can dive from as high as 98 feet (30 m) in the air. It travels about 62 miles (100 km) an hour on its way down to the ocean. That's as fast as a car. The birds hit the water so hard that they often plunge at least 30 feet (9 m) below the surface.

Hitting the water that hard should hurt or kill the bird. So why don't the gannets get hurt? Gannets have special air sacs in their chests. These cushion their bodies when they hit the water. They also have special flaps to close their nostrils and keep water out.

A gannet is like a missile hitting the water!

5 The Jaguar

The name "jaguar" may come from a Native American word that means "kill with one leap." That's a great way to describe this powerful cat, which is a top all-around animal athlete.

19

It's a Fact

Jaguars once roamed most of North and South America. Today they are mostly found in small parts of South and Central America.

Jaguars are the largest cat in South America. These cats are top predators. They can run between 50 and 60 miles (80–97 km) an hour over short distances. This speed allows the jaguar to run down and catch its prey. Unlike most cats, jaguars also like water. They are excellent swimmers and can splash along quite quickly.

Quick running and fast swimming help jaguars catch many different kinds of prey. These **carnivores** eat many different animals, including deer, monkeys, sloths, alligators, snakes, fish, and turtles.

Jaguars are very good climbers too. A jaguar can't eat a large animal, such as a deer, all at once. So the cat climbs a tree, dragging its leftover dinner behind it. A jaguar has to be very strong to carry a heavy animal up a tall tree! Then the jaguar stores its meal in the tree, where it is safe from other animals. Those leftovers will make a tasty snack the next time the jaguar gets hungry!

Jaguars spend much of their time in trees.

 The Kangaroo

Lots of animals run and jump. But did you know there is an animal that likes to kickbox? The kangaroo is the champion kickboxer of the animal world!

Kangaroos live in Australia. Male kangaroos often fight with each other. They fight over **territory** or which one will **mate** with a female.

Kickboxing 'roos

When kangaroos fight, they stand up on their back legs and hit and punch each other with their front legs. A kangaroo's legs are very powerful, so fights can get pretty rough! The kangaroo's long tail helps it keep its balance while it boxes.

You talkin' to me?

It's a Fact

Kangaroos live in big groups called mobs or troops.

Kangaroos are also great at jumping. A kangaroo can jump about six feet (2 m) in one leap. But if the animal is being chased, it can leap almost 30 feet (9 m) in one jump. It can also jump as high as six feet in the air and run about 35 miles (56 km) an hour.

Kangaroos are **marsupials**. They are the largest marsupials in the world. Kangaroo babies, or joeys, are tiny when they are born. They crawl into a pouch on their mother's stomach. The joeys stay inside the pouch to nurse and grow stronger. Older joeys often hop out of the pouch, then go back in for a ride. When they are between seven and ten months old, they will leave the pouch for good.

Mom and her joey

3 The Horned Dung Beetle

The horned dung beetle is an insect with super strength! Sure, these insects are small, but one beetle can carry 1,100 times its own weight. If a person did that, he or she could drag six big trucks down the road!

So what do dung beetles carry? Poop! Dung is another word for poop. Horned dung beetles gather up bits of poop they find on the ground. They roll the poop into a big ball. Then they lift up the ball and carry it off to eat. While a poop ball might sound like a nasty snack to you, the beetle  likes it just fine. And since animal poop often contains bits of undigested food, it provides a healthy food for the beetle.

Horned dung beetles live in many different places. They live on every continent except Antarctica and are found in forests, grasslands, and deserts. These beetles lay their eggs underground. The adults come above ground to look for poop to eat. Some beetles find poop by using their sense of smell. Others cling onto the back legs of an animal and wait for the poop to come out.

Males have long horns on their head.

horns

Horned dung beetles don't just get their exercise by carrying poop balls around. The males also fight. Male beetles have horns on their head. They use these horns to battle each other.

2 The Froghopper

The froghopper is a teeny-tiny insect. This creature is about the size of a pencil eraser. But it can jump higher than any other creature. This insect can leap more than two feet (60 cm) in the air! That's about 100 times its length. If a person could jump that high, he or she could leap over a tall building!

Froghoppers jump from plant to plant. They suck the juices out of plants and can do a lot of damage to crops. These insects also feed on grass. They are found all over the world, including Europe, Asia, North America, and Africa.

Look at the insect's head. You can see how this super-hopper gets its name.

What makes the froghopper such a good jumper? Its back legs. A froghopper's back legs have strong muscles that store energy. When the insect is ready to leap, it pushes off the ground with its legs, releasing a powerful burst of energy. A froghopper's jump is so strong, it is 400 times the force of gravity. No other insect or animal has such a powerful jump.

The Cercopideae, shown here, is the largest family of froghoppers.

Froghoppers are sometimes called spittlebugs. When they are young, they secrete a white, foamy liquid from their bottoms. This liquid looks like spit. It covers the insect and hides it from predators who might eat it. The spittle also keeps the young insects wet so they do not dry out in the hot sun.

1 The Cheetah

And now, we present the #1 animal athlete— THE CHEETAH!

Cheetahs are the fastest land animal. These fast cats can run up to 75 miles (120 km) an hour. They can go from 0 to 60 miles per hour in just three seconds. That is faster than most cars. But there is a catch to the cheetah's super speed. It can only run that fast for a few seconds. After that, the cheetah drops back to a walk.

Cheetahs sprint to catch their prey and kill it with a bite to the throat.

A cheetah's super speed helps this cat catch its prey. Cheetahs live in grasslands in Africa. A cheetah will hide in the long grass and wait for an

animal, like an antelope, deer, or rabbit, to come near. When it sees its prey, the cheetah will creep slowly through the grass, getting closer and closer. When it is close enough, the cheetah bursts out of the grass and runs at top speed to bring down its prey.

Just about every part of a cheetah's body helps it run fast. This cat has very long legs that can cover up to 25 feet (7.5 m) in one leap. Its lungs are super-sized to hold a lot of air, and its heart is oversized too. This cat also has flexible hips and spine to help it move quickly. Its long tail helps the cheetah balance as it runs.

Cheetahs also have special claws. Most cats pull their claws in while they run; they stretch them out to grab prey. But a cheetah's claws are always out. This helps the cat grip the ground while it runs and grab hold of its prey.

Cheetahs often live in groups. A mother lives with her cubs until the babies are about two years old. Adult male cheetahs live and hunt together. When these animals aren't racing after prey, they spend most of their time lying quietly in the long grass.

Animal Athlete Runners-Up

Here are a few more creatures that didn't quite make the Top 10, but are still pretty great animal athletes!

Klipspringer

Sailfish

Sea lion

Springtail

What's Your Top 10?

You've seen our list of
the Top 10 Animal Athletes
and some runners-up as well.
Now it's your turn! Which animals
in this book do YOU think are the most athletic? Are there
other animals that you think should be on the list? Check
your library or go on the Internet and find photos and
information on all that's athletic in the animal world.
Then make your own Top 10 list!

Glossary

carnivores animals that eat other animals

compete to challenge another creature in order to win something

extinct no longer alive

flexible able to bend easily

flocks large groups of birds

habitat the place where animals and plants live

mammals warm-blooded animals that have hair, give birth to live young, and nurse their young

marathon a race covering 26 miles and 385 yards

marsupials mammals whose babies are not completely developed when they are born

mate to have babies with another animal

parasites creatures that live off another animal

predators animals that eat other animals for food

prey animals eaten by other animals for food

secrete to produce a liquid

swarm to fly in large numbers

territory an area defended by an animal

Learn More in the Library

Cowley, Joy. *Chameleon, Chameleon.* Scholastic, 2005.

Davey, Owen. *Bonkers About Beetles.* Flying Eye Books, 2018.

Johns, Chris and **Elizabeth Carney.** *Face to Face with Cheetahs.* National Geographic Children's Books, 2008.

Index

Africa 10, 28, 34

Antarctica 26

Asia 10, 28

Australia............... 22

Europe 28

kickbox 22

North America 14, 20

South America 20

synchronized
swimming 8

About the Author

Joanne Mattern is the author of nearly 350 books for children and teens. She began writing when she was a little girl and just never stopped! Joanne loves nonfiction because she enjoys bringing science topics to life and showing young readers that nonfiction is full of compelling stories! Joanne lives in the Hudson Valley of New York State with her husband, four children, and several pets!